Freight Train
Donald Crews

Greenwillow Books

Freight Train. Copyright © 1978 by Donald Crews. All rights reserved. Printed in the United States of America
For information address HarperCollins Children's Books, a division of HarperCollins Publishers, 10 East 53rd Street, New York, NY 10022
www.harpercollins.com First Edition 13 LP 20 19

Library of Congress Cataloging in Publication Data. Crews, Donald. Freight Train. "Greenwillow Books."
Summary: Brief text and illustrations trace the journey of a colorful train as it goes through tunnels, by cities, and
over trestles. [1. Railroads—Trains—Pictorial works. 2. Colors. 3. Picture books] I. Title. PZ7.C8682Fr
[E] 78-2303 ISBN 0-688-80165-X (trade) ISBN 0-688-84165-1 (lib. bdg.) ISBN 0-688-11701-5 (pbk.)

With due respect to Casey Jones, John Henry, The Rock Island Line,
and the countless freight trains passed and passing the big house in Cottondale

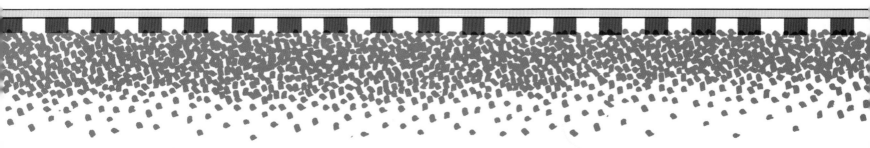

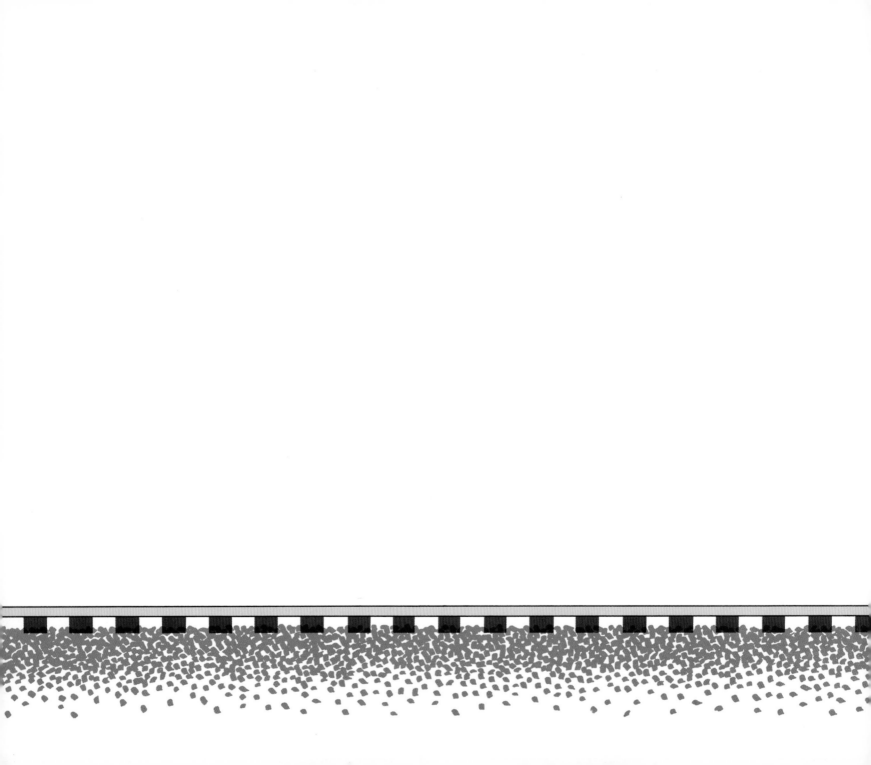

A train runs across this track.

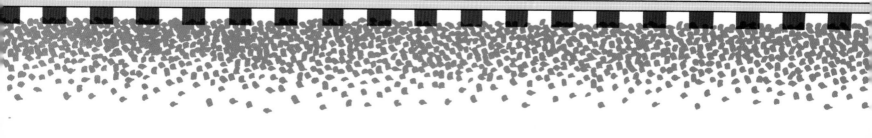

Red caboose at the back

Orange tank car next

Yellow
hopper car

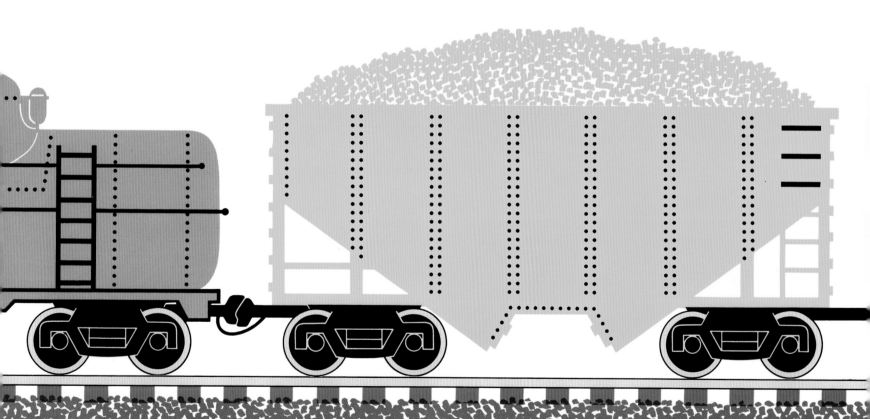

Green
cattle car

Blue
gondola
car

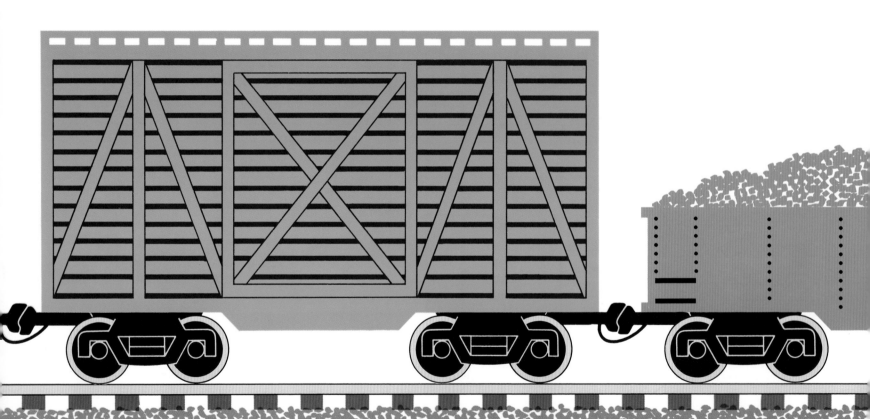

Purple
box car

a Black tender and

a Black
steam engine.

Freight train.

Moving.

Going through tunnels

Going by cities

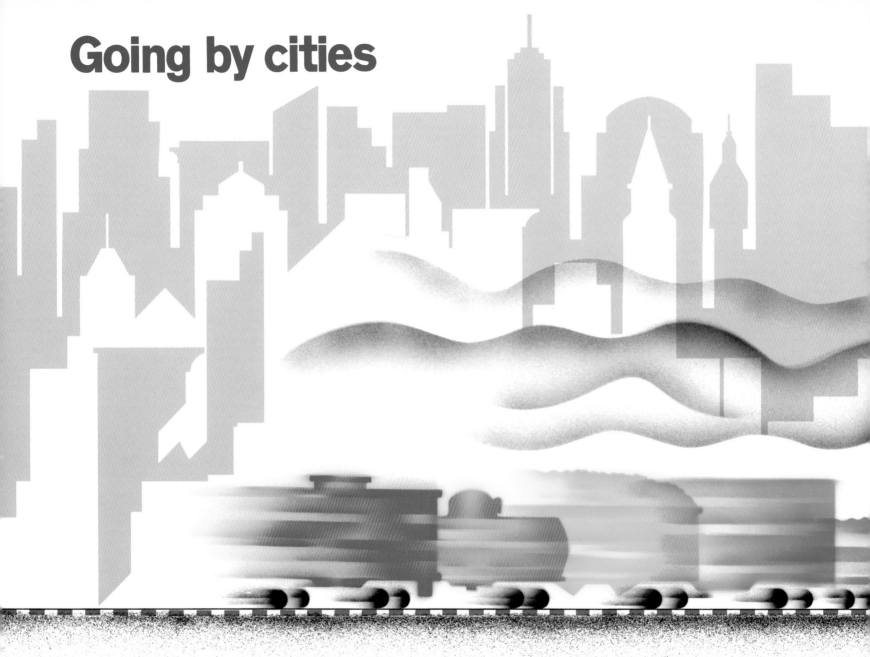

Crossing trestles.

Moving in darkness.

Moving in daylight.
Going, going...

gone.

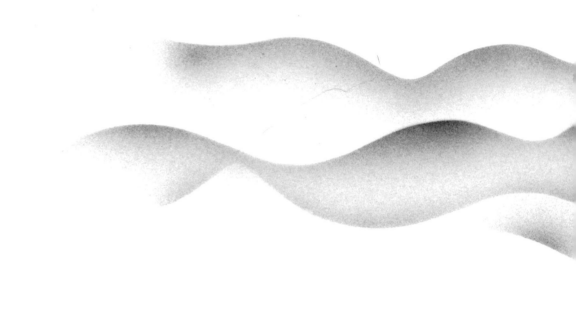